recorder

First American edition, 1988.
Copyright © 1988 by Eric Hill. All rights reserved.
Published simultaneously in Canada.
A Ventura book, planned and produced by Ventura Publishing Ltd.,
27 Wrights Lane, London W8 5TZ, England.
Printed and bound in Singapore by Tien Wah Press (Pte) Ltd.
L.C. number: 88-2500. ISBN 0-399-21563-8.
G.P. Putnam's Sons, 200 Madison Ave., NYC 10016.
10 9

Spot's Big Book of Words

snail

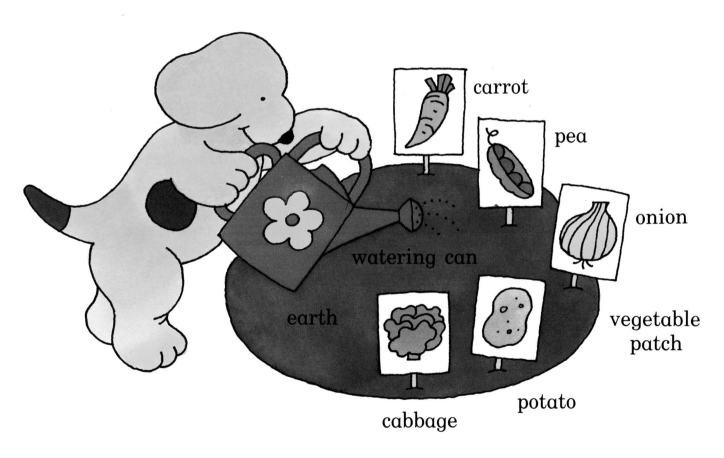

carrot

pea

onion

watering can

earth

vegetable patch

cabbage

potato

Eric Hill

freezer

***

magnets

pitcher

orange juice

coffeepot

refrigerator

coffee

spoon

toast

toaster

It's breakfast time and Spot gets the orange juice from the refrigerator. Sally is making cheese sandwiches for Sam to take to work.

cereal

milk pitcher

bowl

mug

kettle

curtains

window

saucepan

strainer

frying pan

THE NEWS

teapot

eggs

plate

honey

knife

fork

tablecloth

bread knife

bread

stove

cheese

burner

mustard

sandwich

margarine

chimney

roof

farmhouse

sheep

fields

orchard

goose

fence

truck

Spot is helping his dad on the farm. Tom and Helen came along to help, but playing with the wheelbarrow is more fun.

horn

wheelbarrow

pond

duck

rope

ducklings

stake

frog

hoof

clock

blackboard

chalk

teacher

book

bookcase

Spot is at school.
Tom is coloring a picture
with crayons and Spot
and Helen are painting
pictures on their easels.
Soon they will all go
outside to play.

building blocks

ruler

paste

scissors

pencil

eraser

desk

workbook

book bag

crayons

bell

map

slide

swing

seesaw

playground

door

lunch box

thermos

faucet

sink

easel

paper

brush

drip

apron

water jar

red

green

paint box

thumbtack

blue

yellow

keyboard

piano

Miss Bear's class is having a music lesson.
Spot thinks it's all great fun – what a noise they're making!

note

guitar

bow

violin

sheet music

music stand

harmonica

tambourine

triangle

recorder

Next door, Helen and Betsy are having a dance lesson. The teacher is going to play some ballet music on the stereo.

record

stereo

stereo speaker

Swan Lake

record cover

stage

steps

star

wand

spotlight

tutu

wings

barre

fairy costume

ballet shoes

cassette player

tape

Tom is painting the shed while Spot waters the vegetable seeds he has planted. Helen has picked some flowers to take home to her mother.

wall

hedge

gate

bush

path

apple tree

leaf

worm

buttercup

apple

lawn

butterfly

flowers

birdbath

flower bed

basket

shed

roof

shears

brush

hammer

window

shovel

door

paint

fence

hose

bench

rake

flower pot

carrot

pea

snail

onion

fork

watering can

trowel

earth

vegetable patch

seed packet

cabbage

potato

seagull

rod

Spot is at the beach
and can't wait to get
to the sea! Helen, Steve
and Tom are at the beach, too.
What is Helen looking at
through her telescope?

airplan

float

line

pier

hook

seaweed

yacht

waves

hat

fish

surf

telescope

rubber
ring

bucket

anchor

stairs

pebbles

suntan lotion

beach ba

streamer

HELLO, SPOT!

kite

sun

lighthouse

horizon

ship

umbrella

fishing net

rock pool

sand

rocks

sunglasses

spade

sand castle

starfish

seashell

crab

plant

front door

feather
duster

chair

dust

broom

grandfather
clock

staircase

magazine

sofa

cushion

newspaper

It's house-cleaning time and Spot and his friends are helping Sally. Turn off the television, Steve!

curtain

mirror

tulips

television

light switch

vase

telephone

remote control

drawer

lampshade

chest

footstool

table lamp

rug

vacuum cleaner

coffee table

furniture wax

fruit bowl

It's such a fine day! Everyone
is out in the park. Look at
Tom on his new bicycle!

tennis
ball

sun
visor

tennis
racket

net

roller skates

cap

hand
brake

jump rope

handlebars

pedal

tire

bicycle

helmet

elbow pad

knee pad

skateboard

earphone

headband

stopwatch

transistor radio

jogging suit

sock

sole

heel

jogging shoes

trampoline

tricycle

It's Spot's birthday and he has invited his friends to a birthday party. How old do you think Spot is today? Count the candles on the cake!

Happy bi

party hat

horn

ice cream

sandwiches

cookies

sailboat

lid

box

teddy bear

airplane

closet

hanger

cupboard

belts

rail

jacket

skirt

blouse

T-shirt

shoes

party dress

jeans

mirror

purse

drawer

beads

sandal

Helen's mother has
bought a new dress and
sweater for Helen.
Do you like pink?
Helen does!

dress

box

sweater

jacket

overalls

tie

cowboy boot

cap

shorts

duffel bag

pants

moccasins

socks

rugby shirt

shirt

rain hat

boots

suitcase

sneakers

umbrella

swimsuit

Spot is helping Steve pack for a vacation. Steve can't find a pair of socks that match. Look under the drawer, Steve!

Spot and his friends are enjoying some winter fun. Helen made the snowman and his dog. Spot thinks the dog looks like him!

ski poles

goggles

ski boots

skis

mountains

fur hat

frozen pond

snowball

earmuffs

ice skates

mittens

broom

pipe

snowman

scarf

boots

snowdog

snow

smoke

chimney

tree

icicle

log cabin

woolly hat

snowflake

gloves

sled

robin

footprints

log

Spot is staying overnight
at Tom's house.
Tom wants Spot to share the
bunk bed, but Spot pretends
he is camping out in his
sleeping bag and sleeps on
the floor.
Sleep well, Spot!

calendar

MAY

S	M	T	W	T	F	S
1	2	3	4	5	6	7
8	9	10	11	12	13	14
15	16	17	18	19	20	21
22	23	24	25	26	27	28
29	30	31				

pajamas

bulletin board

clock

night table

sheet

blanket

slippers

bunk bed

ladder

pillow

shower curtain

cabinet

hook

toothbrush

shower

bath toy

toothpaste

shower cap

sponge

soap

faucet

radio

toilet paper

sink

towel

bathtub

toilet

bathrobe

bath mat

sleeping bag

zipper

flashlight

backpack

cookies

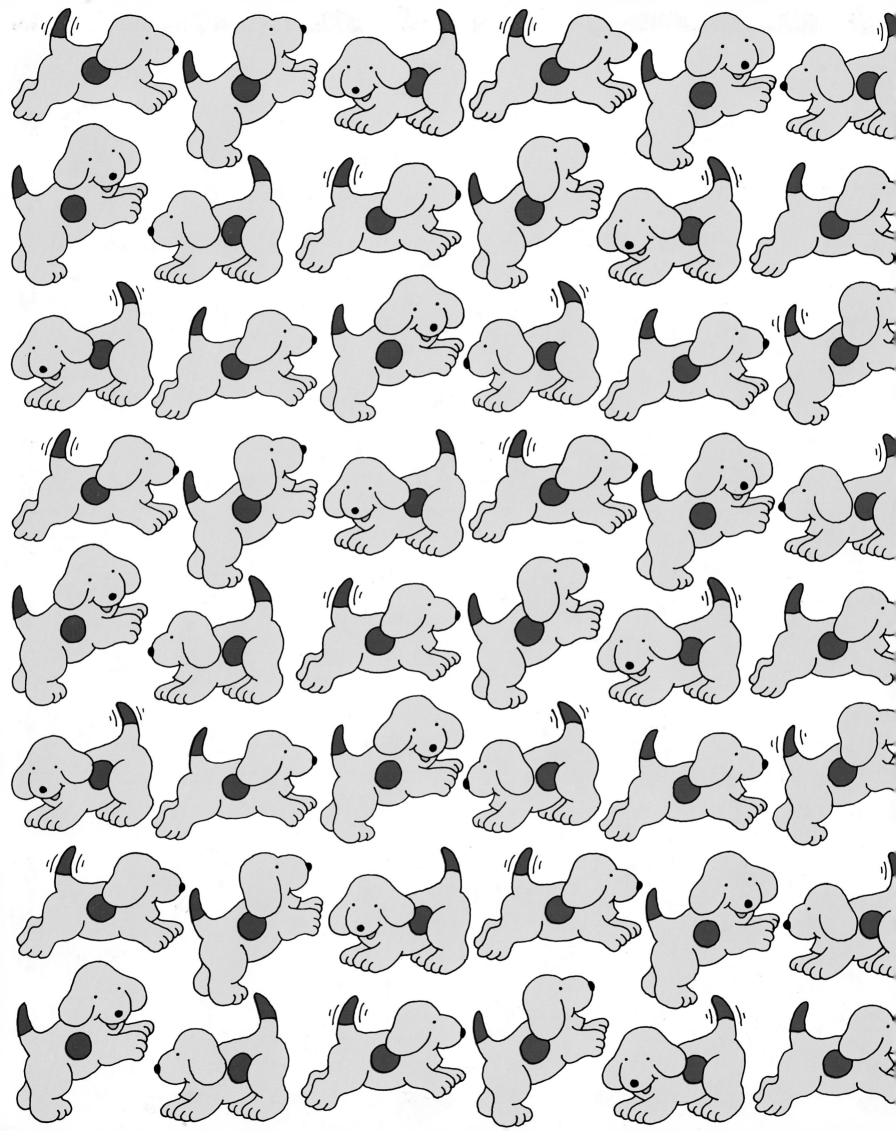